TABLE OF CONTENTS

ANDREW, LOGAN, COACH FRENCH, NOAH, CARLOS

Playbo

WILDCATS FOOTBALL

SEPT. 8 VS. HORTON EE HUSKIES

VS. RIVE ITY CYCLONES

HUSKIES

LIONS

BUCCANEER

CHAPTER 1

IMPROVISED

It was Thursday afternoon. At Westfield Junior High, the eighth-grade Wildcats football team was having practice.

Carlos Suarez, the star quarterback, crouched five yards behind his center for a shotgun snap. "Hut!" he shouted. "Hut!"

After a pause, the center snapped the ball. Carlos caught it perfectly and turned to his right. The running back came around him for the handoff.

Carlos motioned to the running back, but faked the handoff for a play action. He spun to his left, fooling the defense completely.

Carlos looked up the field for a receiver. His best receiver, Andrew Tucker, darted across the field. The defender stuck with him, though.

Carlos looked around the field, trying to find someone to pass to. The other receivers were also having trouble losing their defenders. No one was open for a pass.

Carlos considered the options. *It's only fifteen yards to the end zone,* he thought. *I can do it.* So he ran the ball himself. Some of the defensive linemen were still distracted by the running back. But one defender recovered quickly. He went after Carlos.

Carlos was only five yards from the end zone when the defender caught him. Carlos felt the tackler's arms close around his waist.

But Carlos was just as big as the defender, and he didn't go down. He dragged the tackler right into the end zone with him.

"Touchdown!" Coach French shouted, blowing his whistle. "Nice play, Carlos," he added.

"Thanks, Coach," Carlos said. He walked over to the coach and tossed him the football.

The coach turned to the rest of the team. "Did everyone see how Carlos handled that play?" he asked the team as everyone gathered around.

"It was supposed to be a long play," Andrew said. He pulled off his helmet. Carlos could tell his teammate was angry.

The coach nodded. "Yes, it was," he said. "But the defense was tight on the receivers upfield. Carlos improvised. It was a smart move, and it worked."

Carlos smiled. "Right," he said. "I saw the best move would be to run the ball myself."

Andrew crossed his arms. "Next time, I'll get open," he said. Carlos could tell that Andrew wasn't happy. Carlos seemed like a champion, while Andrew himself had failed in his role as receiver.

The coach blew his whistle. "Okay, everyone," he said. "That's it for practice. We've got a big game tomorrow, so go home and rest up."

"Against the Huskies," Logan Meltzer said. Logan was new to Westfield. He had just moved from River City. Now he was the Wildcats' starting middle linebacker.

"They're pretty tough," Logan went on. "There are some seriously huge guys on that team."

A few people laughed. Logan was one of the strongest guys on the Wildcats. It was funny to hear him call anyone else "seriously huge." Carlos figured the Huskies must be giants if Logan thought they were huge.

"Logan's right," Coach French said. "They are tough. But you guys know that Westfield has a history against the Huskies. As some of you know, the eighth-grade Wildcats football team has never defeated the eighth-grade Huskies."

Carlos smirked. "We can get them this year, Coach," he said. "I'm the quarterback, so they don't stand a chance!"

Andrew rolled his eyes, and Logan laughed.

Coach French turned to Carlos. "You're one of the best QBs we've had, Carlos," he said. "But you're not invincible."

"I'm super quick, Coach," Carlos said. He ran in place and did a few dodges. Some other guys on the team laughed.

The coach shook his head. "These guys are big and fast," Coach said. "You might find running the ball or relying on the short game will be tougher than normal."

Carlos waved the coach off. "They won't be able to catch me," he said. "This will be a piece of cake."

Coach French looked at Carlos for a long moment. "I hope you're right, Carlos," Coach French said. "You'll be calling the plays in the game. Remember to keep your options open, just like you did in practice today. Okay?"

Carlos shrugged. "Sure, Coach," he said.

Coach French shook his head again. Then he looked at the rest of the team. "Okay, boys," he said. "Hit the showers and then head home to rest up for the big game."

He clapped once and patted Andrew on the back. Then the team headed to the locker room.

CHAPTER 2

GAME DAY

The next day was the big game against the Huskies. After their last class, Andrew and Carlos walked together to the locker room. The halls were crowded with people hurrying home for the weekend.

Carlos was all smiles, thinking about the game against the Huskies. He wasn't at all nervous about the game. But Andrew was worried because of what Logan and Coach French had said.

"You heard the coach," Andrew said. "And that new kid, Logan. The Huskies are tough, Carlos!"

"And I'm tough too," Carlos replied. He held out his arm and flexed. "Not to mention fast, smart, and smooth. Those guys don't stand a chance with me as QB."

Andrew shook his head as Carlos stopped at a water fountain for a drink.

"I don't know, Carlos," Andrew said. "I think we should try some of those passing plays we've been practicing. You know I can get open."

"Yeah, you're pretty fast too," Carlos said. He wiped his mouth. "Not as fast as me, but still fast."

"Ha ha," Andrew said. "But passing might be key against the Huskies."

They started walking again. Soon they were at the locker room. Carlos pushed the doors open. Most of their teammates were already there, getting into their uniforms for the big game.

"Listen, Andrew," Carlos said. "Coach French wants me to call the plays. I think the short game is going to be the way to go today."

"I hope you're right," Andrew said. He went to his locker and opened it. "Because I don't want Westfield to lose to the Huskies again this year."

Carlos pulled off his sweater. Then he opened his locker. "Quit worrying, will you?" he said. "It's going to be fine."

CHAPTER 3

LOVE OF THE GAME

The game against the Huskies started at four, right after school. It was early for Friday night football, but the high school team's game would start at seven. The eighth-grade game needed to be over before then.

Carlos was the first person out on the field. He threw his football high and short, then ran ten yards or so and caught it. Carlos liked to get out first to take it all in.

Since it was a Friday, the grounds crew had been out that day, mowing the field and repainting all the yard lines. Carlos loved the smell of the fresh-cut grass. He loved how bright and white the new yard lines were.

But he didn't love anything more than the feel of a football in his hands. Sometimes, he loved that feeling so much, he didn't want to pass the ball or hand it off. He just wanted to keep it and run for the end zone.

While Carlos threw the ball around by himself, the rest of the Wildcats showed up at the field. Soon, the Huskies' bus arrived in the parking lot.

Carlos watched as the other team marched to their bench.

The Huskies uniform was silver and white, with black numbers. Their helmets were silver, too, with a picture of a black dog, howling.

The game would be starting soon. Carlos took a deep breath and headed over to his team's bench. As quarterback, he felt the pressure of this game. He knew it was up to him to end their losing streak against the Huskies.

Before the game-opening kickoff, Coach French gathered everyone in a huddle by the bench.

"All right, everyone," he said. "Let's look alive out there. Remember, Carlos will be calling most of the plays."

Andrew looked at Carlos. Carlos tried to ignore his teammate's stare.

The coach went on. "Carlos, we all know you're strong in the short game," he said. "But remember, if you need to pass, pass."

"I know, Coach," Carlos said. Then he smiled and added, "But I really doubt I'll need to."

Coach patted him on the shoulder. "Okay," he said, "on three, break. One, two, three . . ."

"Break!" the whole team shouted. The kickoff-return team ran out to the field.

Andrew caught the kickoff at the ten-yard line. He cut toward the sideline, then dodged back toward the center. After losing two Huskies, he was finally tackled at the forty.

"Nice return, Andrew," Logan said as they jogged off the field.

Carlos gave Andrew a high five. "Good run," Carlos said. "Now let's see what I can do with it."

Logan rolled his eyes and sat on the bench. Andrew and Carlos headed out to the forty-yard line for first down.

In the huddle, Carlos called a handoff to the running back, Kyle Aaronson. Then Carlos clapped, and everyone in the huddle shouted, "Break!"

Carlos took the snap at shotgun. Then he spun right and handed the ball off to Kyle.

Kyle came around to the left side behind the line. Then he started running up the sideline as fast as he could. But he wasn't quick or big enough to get past the Huskies linebackers.

Kyle was knocked out of bounds. He hadn't even crossed the scrimmage line.

"Loss of three yards," the referee called after blowing his whistle. "Wildcats on the thirty-seven. Second down!"

Carlos shook his head. "You have to shake those guys, Kyle!" he said when the team was back in the huddle. "Okay, let's try the same thing, other way, but play action. I'll run it through the middle when the linebackers come after you, Kyle. Everyone got it?" When everyone nodded, Carlos said, "Okay, break!"

Carlos got into shotgun again. "Hut!" he yelled.

The Huskies middle linebacker laughed. "Are these guys doing another handoff?" he said.

Carlos took the snap and spun to his left. He faked the handoff to Kyle.

But it didn't work. Soon every Huskies player was chasing Carlos. He never even got across the line of scrimmage.

The referee blew his whistle. "Loss of two yards," he said. "Third down, Wildcats ball."

Andrew helped Carlos up. "This is a pretty slow short game we're playing right now," he said.

Carlos shook him off. "Don't worry about it," he said. "We're softening them up. It's still early."

Everyone headed back to the huddle. Andrew slowly joined them. "I hope you're right," he mumbled to Carlos. "I really hope you're right."

CHAPTER 4

LOSING

Toward the end of the first quarter, the score was still 0-0. After a Huskies punt to the forty-five, it took the Wildcats two downs to get the ball to the fifty.

In the huddle before third down, Carlos called the first Wildcats passing play. "Let's try a screen to Kyle out to the right," Carlos said. "Play action, I'll roll left and then throw to you, Kyle. You should be wide open if I can keep them on me."

"Okay," Kyle said, but he sounded worried. He hadn't gotten more than a yard or so against the Huskies yet. They were just too tough.

"Okay, break," Carlos said. He was starting to sound tired.

Carlos took the snap from shotgun again. He rolled to the left and faked the handoff to Kyle.

The Huskies middle linebacker shouted, "Play action!"

Carlos had been hoping they'd spot the fake, though. He ran to the left sideline and immediately turned and threw the screen pass to Kyle.

But Carlos hadn't been quick enough. The Huskies defensive line was on Kyle in an instant.

Kyle fell at the scrimmage line for no gain. Carlos hurried to the huddle.

"Are we going for it, Carlos?" Kyle asked when the huddle was together again.

Carlos shook his head. "Nope. It's way too risky," he said.

"A quick pass over top and we can get the five we need for first down," Andrew said.

Carlos thought a second. Then he shook his head. "No, that's too risky too," he said. "We'll punt."

Carlos waved to the sidelines, and the punting team came in.

It was a good punt, and the Huskies started on the ten-yard line. The Huskies running game was strong, though, and they converted for two first downs.

Soon, they were in range for a touchdown.

"Come on, defense!" Coach French called out. "Force the field goal!"

But the Huskies offense was too tough. Logan did his best to get to their quarterback, but he was too late. The Huskies completed a pass right in the end zone for the touchdown to end the first quarter.

Everyone on the bench moaned.

"That's okay," Andrew said. "That was only one quarter. We can easily come back."

But not one person on the team looked sure.

CHAPTER 5

THE SECOND QUARTER

The referee called the players on for the start of the second quarter. Carlos started to head for the field, but Coach French grabbed his arm.

"What's up?" Carlos asked.

"Are you still confident in the short game, Carlos?" Coach French asked.

Carlos nodded. "Yeah, Coach," he said. "They're starting to soften in the middle. We can pull this out."

The coach sighed, then patted Carlos on the back. "Okay, Carlos," he said. "I'm trusting you because you're my star quarterback. But you'll have to prove you can call these plays."

After the kickoff, Carlos went out to the huddle for the first Wildcats possession of the second quarter.

The pressure's really on now, he thought. *I have to stop relying on Kyle.*

The rest of the offense waited for him in the huddle. *You know the old saying,* he thought. *If you want something done right, you have to do it yourself.*

Carlos reached the huddle. "I'm going to run it myself," he said. "Break."

The other players looked at each other as Carlos got into shotgun position.

"Hut," Carlos said. "Hut!"

He caught the snap. He quickly faked left toward Kyle and then ran beside Kyle toward the right side. The defensive line followed them.

Carlos started running upfield, and Kyle threw one block. It let Carlos make it past the line of scrimmage for a gain of five yards. The players on the bench clapped and hollered.

Carlos jogged back to the huddle. "Same again," he said quickly. "Break!"

The Wildcats ran the same exact play, and the Huskies didn't expect it. Carlos gained eight yards on the run. The Wildcats had their first conversion of the game.

"Good job, Carlos!" Coach French called from the bench.

Back in the huddle, Carlos looked at Kyle. "Great blocks," Carlos said. "This time we go left."

"Okay," Kyle replied.

Carlos felt the eyes of the rest of the offense on him. "Break!" he said.

As the team lined up, Andrew went over to Kyle. "Why does Carlos think you're the only players on the team?" Andrew asked.

Kyle just shrugged. "I don't know," he said. "I'm not the one calling the plays."

Carlos caught the snap. Kyle came up behind him and turned around. Then the two of them ran toward the left sideline.

The Huskies line had had enough, though. They rushed through the blockers and tackled Carlos ten yards behind the line of scrimmage.

Carlos got to his feet and threw down the football. "Man!" he shouted as the ball bounced on the field.

The referee blew his whistle. "Second down, Wildcats ball," he said. Then he said quietly to Carlos, "Watch that temper, quarterback. Okay?"

"Sorry," Carlos said, but he couldn't help being upset.

The next two downs didn't go well either. Carlos tried running again and got nowhere. On third down, he tried a screen pass to Kyle, but it was incomplete.

"Are we punting?" Kyle asked.

Carlos shook his head. "No way," he said. "I'm not giving up now."

"Carlos!" Coach French called out. "Why aren't you calling in the special team?"

Carlos ignored him. "I'm taking it up the middle," Carlos said. "I need excellent blocking."

He looked at his offensive line. "Don't fail me, okay?" he said. Everyone in the line grunted, but it seemed impossible to run twenty yards against the Huskies.

Carlos called, "Break!" The team got into a tight-snap formation.

Carlos took the snap, and the line tightened around him to block. Carlos managed to push through the crowd of offense and defense for a gain of seven yards, but it wasn't nearly enough.

CHAPTER 6

BIG TROUBLE

Carlos got up and angrily pulled off his helmet. But he wasn't the only angry person on the field. Andrew glared at Carlos, and Coach French was steaming at the bench, pacing back and forth. Carlos groaned.

"You should have called for the punt, Carlos," Andrew said, walking over to Carlos. "You need to stop hotdogging out there."

"Who's hotdogging?" Carlos replied. He got in Andrew's face. "You just can't ever get open."

"Whatever," Andrew said, turning away. "If you keep trying to make every play by yourself, we'll never score." Then Andrew quickly walked over to the bench and sat down.

Carlos headed to the bench too. Coach French was waiting to talk to him.

"Carlos!" the coach snapped. "Why didn't you call the punt? That was an impossible first down."

Carlos sheepishly looked down, frowning. "I thought I could make it," he said. Then he threw his helmet down and sat on the bench to watch the Huskies' possession.

The Huskies were on the Wildcats'
forty-yard line, and the first half was
almost over. After the snap, the Huskies
quarterback rolled out right. He had all the
time he needed to let his receivers get open.
His offensive linemen were just too big and
fast to get past.

Finally he launched the ball twenty-five
yards. The Wildcats tackled the receiver
right away, but it was a big gain and first
down.

On the next play, the Huskies
quarterback made a play action pass right
up the middle for a short gain. But they
didn't need a very big gain.

Going into second down, the Huskies
were only ten yards from the end zone and
another seven points.

"Look alive out there, defense!" Coach French shouted from the bench. Carlos paced back and forth behind him.

On second down, the Huskies running back took a handoff up the right side. Logan got a hand on him at the line for a tackle. The Huskies were only one yard from another TD. "Third down, on the one," the referee called out.

The Huskies came out of their huddle and lined up. "Hut!" the Huskies quarterback said. "Hut!" And the center snapped the ball.

The Huskies quarterback, who looked just as big as the rest of his team, launched himself right over the line for a quarterback sneak. It was another touchdown for the Huskies. After the extra point, it was 14-0 at halftime.

CHAPTER 7

HALFTIME

The Wildcats gathered on the benches in the locker room during halftime. Coach French looked at the ground and shook his head. Andrew glared at Carlos. The whole team looked upset. Everyone sat on the benches, slouched over, with their heads hanging low. Carlos felt like a complete loser.

"Well, that was a rough first half," the coach said. "If we don't change our strategy, we don't stand a chance."

"That's what I've been saying," Andrew said under his breath.

"I don't get it!" Carlos said. He stood up. "Why isn't the running game working? It always works for us."

"No plan ever works all the time, Carlos," Coach French replied. "Sometimes you have to change your plan."

"Obviously, this is one of those times," Logan said with a chuckle. A few other guys laughed. But Carlos didn't.

"I don't know," Carlos said.

"If you're going to be a good quarterback, and not just a superstar," the coach said, "you have to be able to use your teammates' strengths, not just your own."

"What do you mean?" Carlos asked.

"I mean, look for Andrew out there, for example," the coach replied. "This is a team, and everyone has his own skills. We have the players for a great passing game."

"Yeah," Andrew added, "if you think you can connect."

"Hey!" Carlos shot back. "I'll have no problem finding you if you can get open."

"Oh, I'll get open," Andrew replied. He jumped to his feet and stared Carlos down.

"Okay, guys," Coach French said. "Save that attitude for the field."

"Everyone huddle up," Carlos said. "On three, teamwork," Carlos said. He glanced at Coach French. The coach smiled and joined the huddle. "One, two, three . . ."

"Teamwork!"

CHAPTER 8

PASSING GAME

The second half opened with a Wildcats kickoff. The Huskies returned the ball to their own thirty-yard line.

"Come on, D!" Carlos shouted from the bench.

On the Huskies' first down, they managed to gain three yards on a handoff.

"That's all right," Coach French shouted. "Hold them there."

The Wildcats defense was feeling good. When the Huskies snapped again, they rushed. The quarterback went down behind the line, for a loss of three yards.

On third down, the Huskies tried for a short pass to convert, but it was incomplete. They were forced to punt.

Andrew returned the punt to midfield, and the Wildcats offense took the field. In the huddle, Carlos pointed at Kyle. "Handoff," Carlos said.

"What?" Andrew snapped. "After what the coach just said?"

"Trust me," Carlos replied. "Break!"

Carlos took the snap and went to handoff to Kyle. But he faked the handoff and ran left. The Huskies line took him down with a one-yard loss.

"This quarterback is a joke," the Huskies middle linebacker shouted. "He just keeps trying to run. Doesn't he see he can't get past us?"

The other Huskies linebackers grunted and bumped helmets. Carlos could tell they were feeling pretty confident.

Carlos got to his feet and glared at the linebacker. Andrew put a hand on his shoulder. "You ready to pass yet?" he asked.

Carlos laughed. "Huddle up," he said.

In the huddle, Carlos turned to Andrew. "Play action, I'll roll out and find Andrew," Carlos said. "Get open, and cut across midfield, okay?"

Andrew nodded.

"Break!"

Carlos took the snap in shotgun. He rolled to his left and faked the handoff to Kyle. Kyle bolted for the right sideline as Carlos rolled out to the left.

"Play action!" the Huskies linebacker shouted. The defense came at Carlos as he scanned upfield for Andrew.

As he looked, Andrew faked long and cut left toward the middle of the field. Carlos pulled back and launched a perfect spiral up the middle.

Andrew's defender was left in the dust as the wide receiver caught the pass. He turned up field and ran easily. Touchdown!

CHAPTER 9

TEN POINTS DOWN

The Wildcats kicked the extra point to make the score 14-7. On the kickoff, the Huskies ran up to their own forty-yard line.

The Wildcats defense took the field.

The Huskies were angry now. They hadn't wanted to give up even one point. So far, the second half wasn't going so well.

The Huskies quarterback shouted the signals from shotgun formation.

The center snapped the ball. The quarterback spun out to the left and handed off to their running back. Logan tried to get to him, but wasn't quick enough. The Huskies running back almost made it to the fifty before the Wildcats defense could get him down.

On second down, the quarterback took a tight snap. He connected with a short pass right over the line. The receiver ran the ball all the way to the thirty. It was first down.

The Huskies were feeling better now. They were within field goal range, and it was first down.

The Huskies quarterback took the snap and faked handoff. He rolled out to the right and passed. It was incomplete. The Huskies quarterback shook his head and went back to the huddle.

On second down, the Huskies went for another pass. But the Wildcats defense knocked the pass to the ground for another incomplete.

The Huskies were still ten yards from a first down. If they didn't make it this time, they would have to kick the field goal.

"Break!" the Huskies quarterback shouted. They lined up in shotgun formation.

"Hut!" the quarterback called. "Hike!"

He caught the snap and handed off to the running back. The back ran for the right side and cut up the field.

Logan was on him right away. The Huskies running back was down at the twenty-eight.

"Good job, D," Coach French called out.

The Huskies kicking team came in for the field goal. After the snap, the Wildcats defense pushed into the line and jumped, trying to block the kick. But the ball sailed over them and went through the uprights.

The Huskies made the field goal to bring the score to 17-7. The Wildcats would still need to score twice to take the lead or even tie up the game. They only had the fourth quarter left.

CHAPTER 10

TWO-MINUTE WARNING

The fourth quarter dragged on as the two teams fought for every yard. With two minutes left, the Wildcats were still down by ten points. It was third down, and they were on the fifty.

"Okay, Andrew," Carlos said. "This is when it counts. Let's go for that long pass. Play action," he went on, "and I'll hit you at the sideline at their twenty-five. You take it home."

"Will do," Andrew said, smiling behind his helmet.

"Break!"

Carlos took the snap and spun to his right. Kyle came around behind him for the fake handoff. The Huskies line shifted to follow Kyle as Carlos ran toward the sideline and found Andrew.

He pulled back and launched the ball straight up the sidelines as Andrew cut to lose his defender. It was good!

Andrew stopped before the boundary and darted up the field. His defender couldn't keep up. Andrew crossed the line. Another touchdown!

The Wildcats bench went crazy. But it wasn't over yet. Coach French called the team to the bench.

"We're still down by three, boys," the coach said. "Hold them tight on defense. Then, if we can get close enough, let's get the field goal and finish these Huskies off in overtime."

"Okay, Coach," Logan said.

The Huskies returned the kickoff to the forty. On their first offensive play, though, Logan burst through the line and sacked their quarterback. He fumbled the ball, and Logan scooped it up.

The entire Huskies offensive line was on top of him instantly, but the Wildcats had possession at the Huskies' twenty-five.

Now it was up to Carlos and the offense to score. But there was only time for one play!

CHAPTER 11

ONE
LAST PLAY

The offense took the field. Carlos called everyone into the huddle.

"Okay, guys," Carlos said. "In the second half, we've been using the passing game, and it's been great."

Andrew smiled. "That's right," he said.

"Now, we need only twenty-five yards, and they'll be expecting us to pass," Carlos went on.

"Aren't we going to pass?" Kyle asked.

Carlos looked at Andrew, then at Kyle. "I think it's time for me to go back to my skills, guys," Carlos said. "Here's the plan."

Carlos filled the team in on his plan. Then they took the field. When play began, Carlos took the snap in shotgun position. He spun to his left, where Kyle was passing him. Carlos faked the handoff and lowered the ball beside his left leg. The defense couldn't see it there.

Kyle ran right, pretending that he had the ball, and drew two Huskies linebackers off the play. Meanwhile, the safeties up field were sticking tight to Andrew, just like Carlos thought they would be. The Huskies whole defense was busy covering Kyle and Andrew.

Carlos was open to run. He cut up the left side of the field.

The Huskies linebackers finally caught on to what was happening and tore after him.

Meanwhile, the play clock reached zero. If Carlos didn't make it, the Wildcats would lose to the Huskies yet again!

But Carlos was too quick, and the linebackers were too far away. Carlos made it into the end zone before any Huskies could even touch him.

Carlos held the football up and cheered. The rest of the offense ran over and knocked him down in celebration. Everyone was happy and excited.

"Great play, Carlos," Coach French said. "You called a bootleg, saw your options, and made the best choice."

Andrew nodded. "I couldn't shake those safeties," he said. "Great call, Carlos. We finally beat the Huskies."

Carlos pulled off his helmet. "Thanks," he said. "I guess I'm not interested in being a superstar quarterback. I'm just happy to be a good quarterback."

THE AUTHOR
ERIC STEVENS

ERIC STEVENS LIVES IN ST. PAUL, MINNESOTA WITH HIS WIFE, DOG, AND SON. HE IS STUDYING TO BECOME A TEACHER. SOME OF HIS FAVORITE THINGS INCLUDE PIZZA AND VIDEO GAMES. SOME OF HIS LEAST FAVORITE THINGS INCLUDE OLIVES AND SHOVELING SNOW.

15

WHEN SEAN TIFFANY WAS GROWING UP, HE LIVED ON A SMALL ISLAND OFF THE COAST OF MAINE. EVERY DAY UNTIL HE GRADUATED FROM HIGH SCHOOL, HE HAD TO TAKE A BOAT TO GET TO SCHOOL! SEAN HAS A PET CACTUS NAMED JIM.

24

THE ILLUSTRATOR
SEAN TIFFANY

GLOSSARY

confident (KON-fuh-duhnt)—having a strong belief in your own abilities

distracted (diss-TRAKT-id)—not concentrating on what you were doing

impossible (im-POSS-uh-buhl)—something that cannot be done

improvised (IM-pruh-vized)—doing the best you can with what is available

invincible (in-VIN-suh-buhl)—a person who cannot be defeated or beaten

motioned (MOH-shuhnd)—told someone something by using a movement

options (OP-shunz)—something that you can choose to do

possession (puh-ZESH-uhn)—when one team is in control of the ball

DISCUSSION QUESTIONS

1. Andrew accuses Carlos of showing off. What do you think? Was Carlos showing off or just trying to win?

2. Do you think it's more important to be a star or to help your teammates win?

3. Should Coach French have done anything differently in this book?

WRITING PROMPTS

1. Write about a time you felt like a loser. What happened? Why did you feel like that?

2. Do you belong to a team? What do you think is your best teamwork strength? Write about your answer.

3. What do you think happens at the next Wildcats game? Write a description.

MORE ABOUT QUARTERBACKS

In this book, Carlos Suarez is the quarterback for the Westfield Wildcats. Check out these quick facts about quarterbacks.

- The quarterback is the leader of the offensive team and is one of the most important players on a football team.

- Quarterbacks are often responsible for calling offensive plays.

- Quarterbacks do not leave the field during offensive play except in the case of injury or if a game's outcome is sure.

- Famous quarterbacks have included Troy Aiken, Joe Montana, Tom Brady, Johnny Unitas, Joe Namath, Brett Favre, Eli Manning, Peyton Manning, John Elway, and Tony Romo.